Dollie Radford

A light load

Poems

Dollie Radford

A light load
Poems

ISBN/EAN: 9783337206444

Printed in Europe, USA, Canada, Australia, Japan

Cover: Foto ©Andreas Hilbeck / pixelio.de

More available books at **www.hansebooks.com**

A LIGHT LOAD · POEMS BY
DOLLIE RADFORD · WITH DE-
-SIGNS BY BEATRICE E. PARSONS·

The love within my heart for thee
Before the world was had its birth,
It is the part God gives to me
Of the great wisdom of the earth.

PUBLISHED BY ELKIN MATHEWS
VIGO STREET · LONDON · W · 1897

CONTENTS

SPRING SONG

AH love, the sweet spring
blossoms cling
To many a broken wind-
tossed bough,
And young birds among
branches sing,
That mutely hung till now.

The little new-born things which lie
In dewy meadows, sleep and dream
Beside the brook that twinkles by
To some great lonely stream.

And children, now the day is told,
From many a warm and cosy nest,
Look up to see the young moon hold
The old moon to her breast.

Dear love, my pulses throb and start
To-night with longings sweet and new,
And young hopes beat within a heart
Grown old in loving you.

SONG

F I were in the valley-
    land,
And you far up the
    mountain blue,
Would you just turn and
    wave your hand,
And bid me strive to follow you?

If I were in the tossing sea,
    And you upon the quiet shore,
Would you send out your help to me,
    And bid me to my life once more.

If I were cast from Heaven's gate,
    And you within so glad and fair,
I know you would come forth and wait
    Beside me, love, in my despair.

IF I WERE CAST FROM HEAVEN'S GATE

MY SWEETHEART

MY sweetheart lays her hand in mine
   When she would have me glad,
She sings and sings, she never knows
   What music makes me sad.

My sweetheart holds my heart to hers
   When she would have me rest,
She never hears the heavy sigh
   Which breaks within my breast.

Her sweet lips press my tired lids
   When she would have me sleep ;
Alas, they have no power to stay
   The burning tears I weep.

SONG

BELOW the rocks where the sam-
    phire blows,
The pebbled beach in an inlet shows
A quiet cave, where a green fern grows
       By the summer sea.

'Twould cheer and brighten my home
    alway,
But fades if far from the fresh sea spray,
It could not live for a single day
       In the town with me.

Below the hill where the heather lies,
A maiden sings, and her smiling eyes
Say love's a blossom that never dies,
       By the town or sea.

SONG

SHE comes through the meadow
    yonder,
  Her face is turned to the west,
And I divine how her clear eyes shine
  With the light of a lasting rest ;
And the rays of the sun-set wander
  To bless her, and she is blest—

By touch of their golden splendour,
  By beauty of earth and sky,
Her spirit waits at the western gates,
  No music can pass her by
That Heaven or Earth may send her,
  I watch where I stand, and sigh.

8

SONG

A MID a crown of radiant hills,
 A little wood with blossoms rare
Breathes sweetly, while the young lark
  trills
His new learnt melody and fills
  The fragrant air.

Among its boughs the fresh winds play,
 And, where the spreading branches
  part,
The sun-light drops from spray to spray,
And seeks the ferny streams which stray
  Within its heart.

And there the wild bee fills his cells,
 And murmurs through the golden
  hours,
And charmèd fancies and sweet spells,
Are woven in the tall blue-bells
  And cuckoo-flowers.

9

There many a mossy bank entwined
   With shining leaves awaits our choice,
Come swiftly, love, my soul unbind
With thy dear looks, that it may find
   Its prisoned voice.

IN YONDER BAY

IN yonder bay the waves find rest,
  They die along the great shore's
    breast,
      With one low sound

Of longing for the fuller breeze
Which rode across the trackless seas,
  And swept them round.

Ah, love, if I might find their rest,
Might end my wanderings on thy breast,
  I should not sigh

For fuller life, so I might stay
My heart's throb on thy heart some day,
  Before I die.

SONG

HEN first I saw your face,
    love,
    I knew my search was
    done,
    You passed my lonely
    place, love,
The light I sought was won,
When your steadfast eyes looked down
   on me,
And I arose to follow thee.

And something in your smile, love,
   I knew to be a part
Of joy that for a while, love,
   Had slumbered in my heart :
To what sweet music it awoke,
When first you turned to me and spoke!

YOUR STEADFAST EYES LOOKED DOWN ON ME
AND I AROSE TO FOLLOW THEE

SONG

I AM wanting to send you a song, love,
    From over the sea,
But the way, Oh the way is so long, love,
    Between you and me,
All the music would die,
In the waves and the sky,
    Before it reached thee.

I am wanting to tell you my love, love,
    But you will forget
How you lifted your sweet eyes above,
     love,
    How their lashes were wet
When you wished me good-bye,
While the stars filled the sky,
    And my sad sails were set.

SONG

THE birds sang from the tree,
    " Sweetheart
Go forth across the silent hills,
For, in the vale their shadow fills,
Thy love awaiteth thee
      With lonely heart."

She wound a wreath of flowers
      So sweet,
And, while the birds still sang their song,
Across the hills, she passed along
In the fair sunrise hours,
      Her love to meet.

16

But when the sun, asleep
   At eve,
Lay hid behind a purple cloud,
Each little bird in leafy shroud
Saw her return and weep,
   " And dost thou grieve?"

" Ah no, I am not sad,"
   She said,
" He did not know me when I came,
But I have crowned him all the same,
And how can I be sad?
   My heart is glad."

SONG

LOVE my heart is aching, aching,
   While the soft sea-wind is making
Music in the aspens, breaking
   Silence in my soul.
With its sad-voiced singing blending
With my sighs, while stars befriending,
Beams to mid-night seas are sending
   As they eastward roll.

VIOLETS

VIOLETS, sweet violets,
  I can find the fairest,
In a little ferny glen
  Blossom all the rarest,
I can reach the leafy beds
Where they hide their dewy heads.

From the mossy stones and rocks
  Where the pools are deepest,
I can leap across the stream
  Where the banks are steepest,
And beneath the hawthorn get
Many a scented violet.

SPRINGTIME

I N the distant woods are blowing
 Tender buds and blossoms sweet.
Fragrant leaves and grasses glowing
 From the touch of fairy feet :
In the woods a spirit singing
 Stays and touches every tree,
And to loving branches clinging,
 Flowers open tremblingly.

SONG

WHY seems the world so fair,
   Why do I sing?
Why? in the meadow there
   When it was Spring,
There when all fair things were
   Clearer to see,
All the young dreams I'd lost
   Came back to me.

   *   *   *   *

I may not enter now,
   But there's a Spring
Somewhere beyond the sun,
   So I can sing,
So I can wait and sing,
   While I prepare
My soul to welcome thine,
   When we meet there.

SONG

THE golden gorse and the heather
   Bloom down the whole hill side,
And below in the rocks are lying
  Still pools where the sea-flowers hide.
    And all the day
    The shadows play
In the cliffs and the chasms wide.

The hedges are decked with berries,
   The lanes gleam with yellow and red,
And the pale blue endive blossoms,
  And the golden-rod lifts its head,
    And poppies shine,
    And wild wood-bine
Scents the air round the fern's green
  bed.

And Time passes by like a dream,
   And birds sing the whole day long,
And bright-wing'd insects fill the air
   With murmurs, and flash along
      When the green leaves part,
     And my own heart
Is full of a happy song.

SONG

N the first light of the
    morning,
  When the thrush sang
    loud and clear,
  And the black-bird hailed
    day's dawning,
How I wished my love could hear.

When the sun shone on the sand there,
  And the roses bloomed above,
And the blue waves kissed the land there,
  How I longed to see my love.

Now the birds good night are calling,
  And the moonbeams come and go,
And my tears are falling, falling,
  Because I want him so.

24

When the sun shone on the sand there,
And the roses bloomed above,
And the blue waves kissed the land there,
How I longed to see my Love.

WHAT SONG SHALL I SING?

WHAT song shall I sing to you
    Now the wee ones are in bed,
What books shall I bring to you
  Now each little sleepy head
Is tucked away on pillow white,
All snug and cosy for the night?

Many, many singers now,
  Sing their new songs in the land,
Many writers bring us now
  Many books to understand,
But I can sing, these evening times,
Only the children's songs and rhymes

All the day they play with me,
    My heart grows full of their looks,
All their prattle stays with me,
    And I have no mind for books,
Nor care for any other tune
Than they have sung this golden June.

ON THE MOOR

OUT on the moor the sun is bright,
  And the gorse is yellow,
The sky is blue and the air is light,
  And a little fellow
May walk for miles in the grassy way,
On a holiday.

Out on the moor the wild bee dips
  In the sweet fresh heather,
And through the bracken the young hare
    slips,
  In the autumn weather,
And all around shine the tiny wings
Of a thousand things.

LITTLE MAIDEN

LITTLE maiden, are you lonely,
  Standing there beside the sea,
Are your blue eyes sad or only
  Filled with dreams too fair for me?
Are the summer breezes making
  Fairy music on the sand,
And the quiet ripples breaking,
  From some sea-girt fairy-land?

Ah, the fragrant flowers never
  Fade in that sweet sunny air,
And the fairy people ever
  Send you dreams and fancies rare,
Little maiden, you must only
  Keep your blue eyes clear and free,
And you never will be lonely,
  Standing there beside the sea.

THE SNOW-QUEEN

THE snow-queen passed our way last
    night,
Between the darkness and the light,
And flowers from an enchanted star,
Fell showerlike from her flying car.

And silently, through all the hours,
The trees have borne their magic flowers,
And now stand up with dauntless head,
To catch the morning's gold and red.

HOW gently this evening the ripples
    break
  On the pebbles beneath the trees,
With a music as low as the full leaves
    make,
  When they stir in some soft sea-breeze.

And as day-light dies, if I rest my boat
  'Neath this bough where the blossoms
    fall,
I shall hear the curlew's last good-night
    note,
  As he answers the sea-gull's call.

And there where the wheat lies in golden
    sheaves,
  In the fields across the river,
And wood-bine creeps over porches and
    eaves,
  And fuchsia and myrtle quiver,

32

Lives my love, my love ; 'tis her case-
    ment see,
  Where the light glimmers to and fro,
If she were my love she would come to
    me
  This evening, I long for her so.

I long for her so, that to linger near,
  Her home as I do sometimes,
And send her blessings across from here,
  When they ring the Westleigh chimes.
Makes my summer glad, so I stay my
    boat
  'Neath this bough where the blossoms
    fall,
While the curlew flies with his good-
    night note,
  To the sea where the white gulls call.

COLD STONE

COLD, quite cold, I could only see
  Beauty of curve and line,
I could not find that deeper thing
That secret which dwells in everything,
  I could not make it mine.
The marble stood so cold and still,
  And yet, within her breast,
I knew lay hid a wondrous spell
To open dreams too fair to tell,
  Where I might stay and rest.
I find it ever in the flowers,
  In tints and perfumes sweet,
And in the silent stars at night,
And in the rays of sun-set light,
  Their meaning is complete.
I cried for light to find it here,

And waited, till, one day,
The hand that hid the wondrous gift,
Came from the past the clouds to lift,
And drew the veil away.

TO-NIGHT

THE hours of the day have departed,
    They folded their wings to rest,
When the last red ray of sun-light
    Faded away in the west,
And fleecy clouds cover the stars,
    And beyond is a world of blue,
And my soul awakes from a slumber
    To-night, and I see right through—

Away to a world of azure,
    Where white-wing'd spirits meet,
While the clouds float and fade below
        them,
    And the stars shine at their feet.
They hold out their hands in welcome,
    And now, for a moment of time,
Limitless worlds and boundless space,
    And planets—they all are mine.

EVENING

LISTEN and we shall hear the voice
  Of Evening, her name she told,
When we stayed our boat by the shore
    to know
What wee flower shone 'neath the willow
    so,
  And her hair was radiant gold.

Now veiled in grey with silent step,
  She walks where shades are deep,
And the great trees hear, and the blos-
    soms know,
The song she sings, and her music low
  Is charming them to sleep.

My unseen brother and sister
  Who dwell 'neath the roofs we pass,
Are you sad and weary with toil and care,
My rest is full, I have rest to spare,
  I whisper it through your grass.

OUT ON THE MOOR

I HAVE been wandering to-day
　　Out on the moor, and have seen
The country stretching far away,
　　In stony slopes and wastes of green.

And watched the distant hill-tops lie
　　Far in the sun-set fair and free,
Like purple clouds across the sky,
　　—And further still the line of sea.

And heard the lark above me sing,
　　And seen the plover flying near,
And many a little hidden spring,
　　And twinkling water brown and clear.

And brightest sun, and darkest shower,
　　And day and night-time come to rest,
And toiling wind and tender flower,
　　Upon the moor's untiring breast.

38

We falter in our smiles and tears,
  And faint with joys and sorrows won,
The moors stretch out through all the
      years,
  In perfect peace—till Time is done.

And peace is love, dear love I know
  There is no greater thing than this,
It is the utmost love can show,
  It is the utmost love can miss.

The love within my soul for thee
  Before the world was had its birth,
It is the part God gives to me
  Of the great wisdom of the earth.

WINDS blow cold in the
bright March weather,
Yet I heard her sing in
the street to-day,
And the tattered garments
scarce hung together
Round her tiny form as she turned
away.
She was too little to know or care
Why she and her mother were singing
there.

Skies are fair when the buds are spring-
ing,
When the March sun rises up fresh
and strong,
And a little maid, with her mother, sing-
ing,
Smiled in my face as she skipped along.
She was too happy to wonder why
She laughed and sang as she passed me
by.

TWO SONGS

MY PALACE-HOME

GIVE me thy hand, dear friend, and let
me take thee
Into my palace-home and garden fair,
Beside me follow close, ah, it will make thee
Still dearer, sweetest friend, to see thee
there.

Give me thy hand, dear friend, and let me
show thee
The peaceful resting places in the shade,
Where the stream, flowing pleasantly below
thee,
Stills each unquiet thought the day has
made.

*　　*　　*　　*　　*

No, no, dear friend, my palace-home is lonely,
No hand but mine may pluck the flowers
there,
And, since for me they bud and blossom only,
Thou canst not tell me that they are not fair.

NIGHT

AND art thou come again, Oh Night;
I know thee by thy starry crown,
And by the mists of violet light
Which gather where thy robes fall
down.
I know thee by the purple clouds
Thy strong wings spread around the
moon,
And by the stillness which enshrouds
Thy presence, thou art come too soon.
Too soon, for lo thy fair love sleep
Turns not her sweet face to the skies,
She lingers where the shadows creep,
And stays to kiss our children's eyes.

But when her gentle hands have blest
Our homesteads, she will come to thee,
And through the holy hours of rest
Thine arms will hold her safe, and she
Will hear the promises again
Thou bringest from the distant spheres.

And learn the reason of our pain,
  And meaning of our bitter tears.
Thine eyes are steadfast and I dare
  Their mighty mystery to read,
But mine are dimmed by thought and
      care,
  And fail me in my greatest need.

I watch for thee, wilt thou not bring
  One message to my fainting heart?
Through summer-time and snow and
      spring
  I watch for thee, must thou depart
Thus silently—when will it come,
  That perfect day which we await?
For us thy lips are ever dumb,
  And voiceless is thy calm estate.
Ah! tell thy fair love Sleep, that she
  May touch me when she passes by,
And whisper what she hears from thee
  In some sweet lullaby.

HEART AND HOME

OH, what know they of harbours
    Who toss not on the Sea!
They tell of fairer havens
But none so fair there be,

As Plymouth town outstretching
Her quiet arms to me—
Her breast's broad welcome spreading
From Mewstone to Penlee.

And with this home-thought, darling,
Come crowding thoughts of thee—
Oh, what know they of harbours
Who toss not on the Sea !

46

WHEN YOU ARE LONELY

WHEN you are lonely, full of care,
  Or sad with some new sorrow,
And when your tired fancy hides
  The brightness of the morrow,
Ah, turn your footsteps to the woods
  And meadows, where the rills,
Are quietly flowing, when the moon
  And stars shine on the hills.

Upon your brow the great wise trees
  Will breathe, and something sweet
Will reach you from the fragrant grass
  You press beneath your feet,
And some fair spirit of the fields,
  Peaceful and happy-eyed,
Will find a way into your heart,
  I think, and there abide.

MY FRIEND

THE tender touch of a gentle hand
    To-night on my aching brow,
The sound of a loving low-tuned voice,
    How pleasant they would be now ;
I think they would send the shadows
        away
Which hang so closely around me to-day.

And, sitting idly, I close my eyes
    And dream how perhaps one day,
In my lonely hours, my long-sought friend
    Will come to my home and say :
" Bring all your tired thoughts to me,
        dear, and rest,
No shadow will touch you here on my
        breast."

I shall not tell her, but she will know ;
    My rest will be very sweet,
And all the shadow and gloom will go,
    Caught up in the toiling street ;
And I shall thank her and clasp her hand,
And she will smile and understand.

And if on the morrow we chance to meet
    With others, her face will be
Happy and bright for them all, and just
    A little kinder for me,
And once I shall look in her eyes, and so,
Learn something there no other may
    know.

ORPHEUS

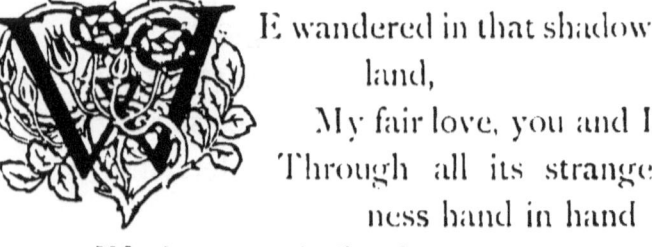E wandered in that shadow-
    land,
  My fair love, you and I,
  Through all its strange-
    ness hand in hand
We journeyed silently.

My lyre is hanging cold and dumb,
  Mute with our triumph song,
I have no voice now you are come,
  Whom I have sought so long.

But I will bring you in Love's land,
  Into Love's highest place,
And crown you there, and understand
  The wonder of your face.

And then my joyous song shall rise
  To sun and moon and star ;
And all the worlds beyond the skies
  Shall tell how fair you are.

ORPHEUS & EURYDICE

BY THE SEA

THE clouds have gathered soon to-
 night,
 They hang above the quiet sea,
And through the air a muffled sound
 Is borne to me.

From that dim island where the souls
 Of all the Ages lie at rest,
It beats upon my throbbing brain
 And troubled breast.

If thou wert standing on the shore
 Beside me now, and held my hand,
I think that I should hear it plain
 And understand.

For there is one note in it all,
 Which loud and clear has come to me,
And I have caught it in my heart
 To tell to thee.

" Eyes steadfast from the watch of worlds,
   Hearts big with secrets of the spheres,
We have no power to move you now
   With hopes or fears."

" No power," thy soul has filled my soul,
   Thy life has rounded all of mine,
Thy love has girt me with a strength
   Which is divine.

And when that sound perchance one day
   Comes to us with a mighty roll,
We two shall stand unmoved, and hear
   And learn the whole.

IN THE WOODS

ARE your grave eyes graver growing?
   Sweetheart, may I look
At the treasured thoughts which move you
   In the poet's book?
Stay not in the lazy shade
   With the drowsy roses;
Come into the woods and see
   Where I find my posies.

Has the buried singer left us
   Songs to make you weep?
Are you saddened by the sorrow
   Which his numbers keep?
Or were all the songs he gave us
   Born in happy hours?
Come with me, he found his music
   Where I find my flowers.

Where a little mossy path-way
　　Lies beside the stream,
Long ago the poet lingered;
　　Sun and pale star-beam
Touched his lips, while there he wan-
　　dered
　　Summer-time and Spring,
And the mighty woods and river
　　Taught him how to sing.

RETURN OF THE TROOPS

THE town is very gay to-day,
　　And down our busy street
Flags wave, and all the balconies
　　Are filled, our men to greet.

One night, not very long ago,
　　I heard them marching down
To where their ship lay, and the sound
　　So filled the silent town

With farewell voices, that I wept
　　To know no word or deed
Of mine had stirred the sleeping night,
　　To bid our men God-speed.

The town is very gay to-day,
　　And, in our busy street,
My eyes are dim with tears for those
　　I neither sped nor greet.

MARCH

THE March wind rises through the
skies,
His great wings rustling as he flies,
And downward sweeps o'er plain and hill
The sunshine to the daffodil.

JUNE

THE skies are blue
   O'er the meadows now,
And the leaves are new
   On the willow-bough,
And the whole earth sings
   In one joyous tune
All the happy things
   Of the happy June.

Oh the golden time
   Of the sweet fresh June,
And the happy rhyme
   Dies away so soon ;
But again—again—
   When the years are young,
Will the sweet refrain
   Be sung—be sung.

CHRYSANTHEMUMS

NOVEMBER with mysterious feet
    Creeps slowly through the land,
And on the bridge and in the street,
Amid the town's tumultuous beat,
    Spreads out a quiet hand ;
And wraps around us unaware
    His mantle grey and cold,
But he has blossoms still to spare,
We find fresh flowers rich and rare,
    Hid in each misty fold.

TO THE UNKNOWN AUTHOR
OF *OBITER DICTA*

JULY, 1884

THOUGH I may rest in some leafy
place,
And read, through the summer day,
Thy pages penned in the busy town—
So busy and far away—
Though hills stretch out, and sunlight
falls
On acres of swelling land,
I seem to span the misty miles
Between us, and clasp thy hand ;
For thou hast bound with magic chain
The vagrant thoughts I chased in vain.

A BRIDE

I SAW your portrait yesterday,
  Set in a golden frame;
Around it twines a blossom-spray,
  Beneath it is your name.

And tender smiles are round your mouth,
  High thoughts are on your brow,
The world is beautiful as Youth,
  You are so happy now.

The shining gates are opened wide,
  Love stretches forth his hand
And bids the bridegroom bring his bride
  Into the promised land.

And you and he dwell there alone,
   Beneath Love's radiant sky,
While all the world's great grief and moan
   As a sad dream pass by.

Yet on Love's flowers strange and rare,
   Your saddest tears may fall,
And in Love's country you may fare
   The loneliest of all.

MY SONGS

THERE is no unawakened string,
   No untried note for me to ring,
No new-found song for me to sing.

Old numbers round my day and night,
When summer comes my heart is light,
'Tis heavy, when the birds take flight.

My love is young, her face is fair,
The sun-light never leaves her hair,
Her beauty fills me with a prayer.

64

And many a tryst and watch I keep,
With those who laugh and those who
    weep,
Between the hours of work and sleep.

The songs I strive to sing have rolled
Through times and ages manifold,
A mighty chorus fully told.

IN OUR SQUARE.

AST night again we saw
him there,
Beneath the plane-tree
in the Square,
Our student neighbour.

He watches every evening now
Our garden tennis, and somehow
It seemed a labour

The running round, and futile stretching
At random balls, while he was sketching
That foolish Polly,

Who quietly stood, with arm up-raised,
The while her junior partner praised
Her style of volley.

I passed so near him as we played,
He looked so peaceful in the shade,
Amid our bustle.

· OUR · STUDENT · NEIGH-BOUR ·

He draws and sketches all the day,
And studies through the night, they say,
      Some bone or muscle.

And is this why his cheek is pale,
And why he looks so thin and frail,
      And is such labour

The reason that his coat is bare,
And worn, and marks him everywhere—
      Our student neighbour?

I know that I shall almost cry
To-morrow when we pass him by,
      All bound together

For Cornish seas, while he—but there
Miss Polly's always in the Square
      This summer weather.

SOLILOQUY OF A MAIDEN AUNT

THE ladies bow, and partners set,
　　And turn around and pirouette
　　　　And trip the lancers.

But no one seeks my ample chair,
Or asks me with persuasive air
　　　　To join the dancers.

They greet me, as I sit alone
Upon my solitary throne,
　　　　And pass politely.

Yet mine could keep the measured beat,
As surely as the youngest feet,
　　　　And tread as lightly.

No other maiden had my skill
In our old homestead on the hill—
　　　　That merry May-time

When Allan closed the flagging ball,
And danced with me before them all,
    Until the day-time.

Again I laugh, and step alone,
And curtsey low as on my own
    His strong hand closes.

But Allan now seeks staid delight,
His son there brought my niece to-night
    These early roses.

Time orders well, we have our Spring,
Our songs, and May-flower gathering,
    Our love and laughter.

And children chatter all the while,
And leap the brook and climb the stile
    And follow after.

And yet—the step of Allan's son,
Is not as light as was the one
          That went before it.

And that old lace, I think, falls down
Less softly on Priscilla's gown
          Than when I wore it.

A MODERN POLYPHEME

A FLASH of colour through the trees,
   A step upon the trembling plank,
A white sail flapping in the breeze,
   And then a maiden leaves the bank.

Each day I watch her, as she guides
   Her little boat with dexterous hand,
And like a river goddess rides
   In gracious triumph through the land.

I watch her as she lightly tacks,
   And marvel at the art which steers
Her boat into the quiet " backs,"
   And sorrow when it disappears.

Who, in the summer evening, knows
   What gentle feelings fill her breast,
Or by what bower the water flows
   Which bears her dingy to its rest?

Perchance a lover, dark and tall,
　Awaits her in some flowery nook,
And gazing at her gathers all
　Her thoughts, as from an open book.

Perchance—I have not learnt her name,
　I know not where her home may be,
For one brief space alone I claim
　Her beauty, as she passes me.

For then the Heaven-winged dreams,
　which smile
And fade in youth's first golden hour,
Come back and soothe my soul awhile
　As the sweet perfume of a flower.

And so I watch for her nor care
　Where Acis tarries down the stream—
Enough to see her, I forswear
　Thy black emotions, Polypheme!

A DREAM OF "DREAMS"

To Olive Schreiner

ALL day I read your book ; at Eve
   Your dreams into my dark sleep
      stole,
Through the unbroken hours to weave
   A picture for my soul.

Now from the deep inspired night
I rise, and, near and stretching far,
I see the earth lie clear and bright
   Beneath one morning star.

The great World-Spirit watching still
Broods over all with folded wings,
And ever down-cast eyes until
   The first bird wakes and sings,

And through the eastern clouds the sun
Breaks with a new unnumbered day
And now His watching is all done—
   The night has passed away.

75

He turns toward the dawn, and I
Wait as he breathes the sweet fresh air,
Then with a new-born joy I cry
    To see His face so fair.

Printed by R. ffolkard & Son,
22, Devonshire Street, Bloomsbury, London, W.C.